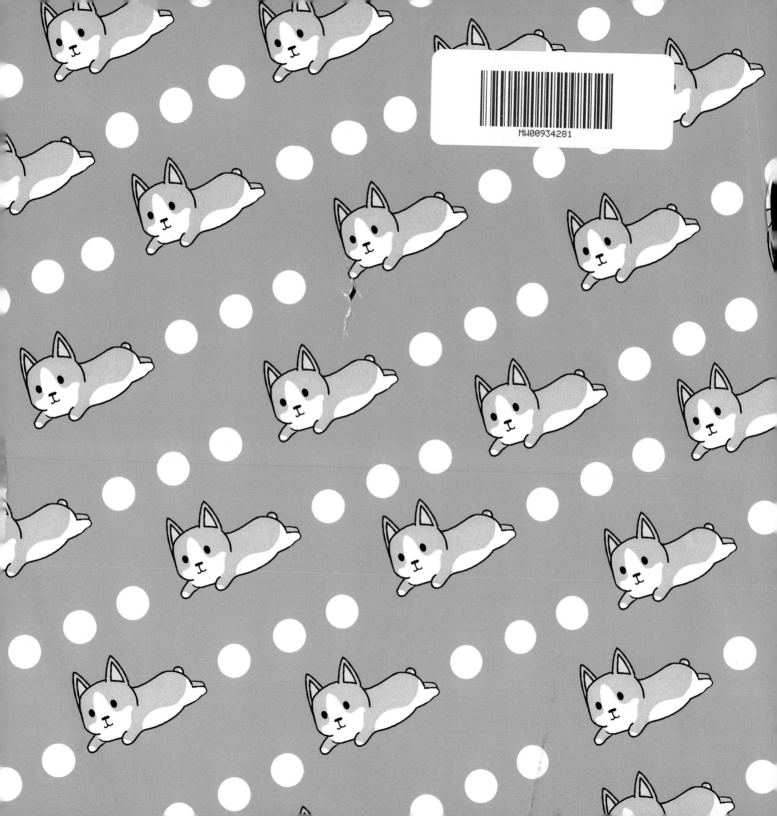

Peaches The Corgi
Who To Be

A Book By : Jessica Sorto

My name is Peaches and I am too small.

When I try to run fast, I trip and I fall!

My legs are too short, with jellybean paws.

I wish I were a cat with kitty cat claws.

I would be a horse with a neck long and tall.

Or maybe a goat who likes to eat straw.

How about a sheep with wool white and soft?

And maybe a cow who eats wheat from the trough.

I could be a pig who has fun in the dirt.

Or maybe my friend who wears a plaid shirt.

But if I was not me, it wouldn't be fun.

I could not chase my tail or run in the sun.

Only I can chew bones and chase chickens around.

And use my great nose to sniff on the ground.

I can dig holes in the grass until the day ends.

Then I get yummy treats from
my plaid shirted friend.

As I lay in my bed, I cannot help but believe.

I'm glad I am me, Peaches the small corgi!

The End

95924008R00015